WITHDRAWN

FOCUS ON THE FAMILY PRESENTS

# *Terror in the Tunnel*

### BOOK 23

**MARIANNE HERING AND SHEILA SEIFERT**
**ILLUSTRATIONS BY SERGIO CARIELLO**

TYNDALE

**FOCUS ON THE FAMILY • ADVENTURES IN ODYSSEY®**
**TYNDALE HOUSE PUBLISHERS, INC. • CAROL STREAM, ILLINOIS**

to Deputy Micah Flick, killed on duty February 5,
2018, and to all law enforcement officers
who daily protect our communities

*Terror in the Tunnel*

© 2019 Focus on the Family

A Focus on the Family book published by Tyndale House Publishers, Inc.,
Carol Stream, Illinois 60188.

*The Imagination Station, Adventures in Odyssey,* and *Focus on the Family* and
their accompanying logos and designs are federally registered trademarks of
Focus on the Family, 8605 Explorer Drive, Colorado Springs, CO 80920.

*TYNDALE* and Tyndale's quill logo are registered trademarks of Tyndale House
Publishers, Inc.

With the exception of known historical figures, all characters are the product
of the authors' imaginations.

Cover design by Michael Heath | Magnus Creative

For Library of Congress Cataloging-in-Publication Data for this title, visit
http://www.loc.gov/help/contact-general.html.

For manufacturing information regarding this product, please call 1-800-323-
9400.

For information about special discounts for bulk purchases, please contact
Tyndale House Publishers at csresponse@tyndale.com, or call 1-800-323-
9400.

Printed in the United States of America

ISBN: 978-1-58997-992-5

25   24   23   22   21   20   19
7    6    5    4    3    2    1

# Contents

# *Prologue*

In book 22, *Freedom at the Falls,* Patrick and Beth had an adventure aboard a passenger train in February 1861. The Lincoln Special was taking President-elect Lincoln to Washington, DC, to be inaugurated. He was to become the sixteenth president of the United States.

That story ended at a bridge over Niagara Falls, New York. Eugene appeared next to the Imagination Station. Here's what happened:

Beth turned toward Eugene. Her mouth fell open in wonder.

"Eugene?" she said. "You look like a teenager! You should be at least thirty years old."

Eugene was an adult friend from Whit's End. He had been with the cousins on their last three adventures. He had looked eighty years old the last time they saw him.

Patrick said, "What happened to you?"

"The appropriate question is, 'What *didn't* happen?'" Eugene said. "I calculated that I would be my proper age in this adventure. But it appears I was mistaken."

"What are you going to do?" Patrick asked.

"Nothing at the moment," Eugene said. "There's something much more important at stake." He paused and took a long breath. "There's a plot afoot to murder Mr. Lincoln. And we have to stop it!"

# The Imagination Station

The wind whipped across the bridge over Niagara Falls. Beth drew the blue cloak tightly around her. She stepped toward Eugene and the Imagination Station.

A teenage Eugene pushed his reddish-brown hair away from his face. His smooth, young skin stretched into a smile.

Beth glanced at the Imagination Station. Had it also changed?

The car was a dark Model T with special pipes, coils, and tubes. The machine looked cleaned and polished. It had a new panel on the trunk.

Eugene nodded. "Mr. Whittaker and I adapted the car at Mr. Tesla's laboratory," he said. "We now have room for four passengers."

He lifted the panel on the trunk. A small seat for two popped up.

"Cool, a rumble seat," Patrick said. "What else is new?"

"Divulging that information would be premature," Eugene said.

"Huh?" Patrick asked.

Beth smiled to herself at Eugene's fancy words. "He means he'll tell us when he's ready," she said.

4

Eugene nodded again. "Let's get inside the Imagination Station," he said.

Patrick said quickly, "I call dibs on the front seat!"

Beth said, "The rumble seat is fine with me." She stepped on the running board and climbed onto the leather bench.

Patrick and Eugene settled in the front seats. Beth noticed that the steering wheel now had a red circle in the center. It looked a lot like the red button on the dashboard of the other Imagination Station.

"Watch this!" Eugene said. He took hold of the steering wheel and turned it. Then he slammed his palm on the steering wheel's center.

*Blatt!*

The horn sounded like a sick duck.

The car seemed to tilt forward. Everything Beth saw through the windshield blurred. She grew dizzy as a million dots of color began to spin.

Then the dots broke apart. They sprayed out of the machine like water droplets.

And then suddenly, everything went black.

# Mr. Davies

Patrick opened his eyes. Darkness surrounded him.

He heard the door on the driver's side of the Imagination Station open. Then footsteps. Next came a faint scraping noise. Suddenly a small, yellowish-orange blur appeared in the room.

Eugene was holding a lit match. He held a thin, white candle in his other hand.

He lit the candle and blew out the match.

Then he moved the candle close to his face. The light gave his skin an eerie glow.

Eugene dropped the burned-out match into an ashtray.

He moved to a table and set the candle in a holder. Then Eugene beckoned the cousins to get out of the Imagination Station.

Patrick hopped out quickly.

After Beth climbed out, the new Imagination Station disappeared.

"Where are we?" Patrick asked Eugene.

"In the home of Captain Ferrandini," Eugene said. "Perhaps I should have explained before we arrived. But now time is of the utmost importance. You two need to hide immediately."

Beth seemed confused. But she slipped behind thick curtains.

Patrick followed. He touched the cool glass doors behind the drapes. Then he looked outside. The moon was almost full. It cast a pale light over a small garden area.

Shrubs surrounded a stone patio and some benches. A few holly bushes had green leaves. A large, bare tree stood in the center of the open space. Its branches went in all directions. Some touched the roof of the house.

"We're in the living room," Beth said.

Patrick turned around. Beth was peeking between the curtains. He peeked out too.

Sofas and couches upholstered in flowers filled the room. Small tables and a few cabinets held vases and books.

Eugene lit more candles. A large, wooden box sat on a table in the center of the room.

Eugene approached the curtains. "Don't let anyone know you're here," he said. "And don't be surprised by anything you see or hear. I've gone undercover. I'm known as Harry Davies and have earned the trust of the captain. The men who are coming think I'm an assassin."

Eugene closed the curtain panels.

A series of soft knocks came from the door.

Patrick gulped. *Eugene a killer?*

# The Baltimore Plot

Several men came into the living room. Their voices were low and serious.

Beth heard Eugene greet a man named Mr. Hillard.

"Mr. Davies," Hillard said to Eugene, "I'm glad young men like you want the South to rebel." The man's voice seemed friendly.

"Weird," Patrick whispered to Beth. "They don't sound like killers."

Eugene greeted other men: a Captain Turner, a Mr. Luckett, and Captain Ferrandini.

"Thank you for preparing my home for this meeting," Captain Ferrandini said. "I was unable to leave work early."

"The pleasure was all mine," Eugene said.

"Ferrandini has an accent," Beth whispered to Patrick. She counted twenty men in the room.

One man praised Maryland: "Our state—nay, our very city of Baltimore—must stop that main traitor Abraham Lincoln."

Another man agreed: "He must not reach Washington. He shall die in this city!"

Cheers erupted. "Hear, hear!" Hoots and hollers filled the room.

Even Eugene's voice sounded gleeful. He said, "We must stop Lincoln at any cost and by any means."

*Eugene is a good actor,* Beth thought. *No one will think Mr. Harry Davies is a spy.*

Suddenly someone said, "And by 'any means,' you are saying, 'death to the president'!"

Beth heard Patrick gulp. She felt a chill travel down her spine. She leaned against the glass door.

*Sque-e-e-ak.*

It swung open toward the garden.

Beth froze in fear.

"What was that?" Captain Ferrandini said. "Have we been discovered?"

Just then a breeze came from the garden. The curtains billowed outward.

*They're going to see us*, Beth thought. *We're doomed!*

# *Eight Red Ballots*

Patrick quickly moved away from the curtain's opening. He pulled Beth with him.

Eugene's form suddenly appeared inside the curtains. He was holding a candle in one hand. With the other, he grabbed the curtain panel to keep it from billowing. No one would see the cousins.

"The door must not have been latched," Eugene said loudly. He grabbed the doorknob and firmly pulled the glass door shut.

Eugene lifted his candle. His eyes reflected the candlelight. They seemed to say, "Be careful."

Eugene slipped back into the living room. The curtain fell straight.

Patrick gave a silent sigh of relief. They were hidden again. He felt Beth relax beside him.

"No one new is here," Eugene said to the men in the room. "It's just the wind."

"Let's hurry with the selection," a man said. "Before our meeting is discovered."

Patrick heard feet shuffling and chairs being moved. He sucked in his breath to gather courage. Then he peeked between the curtain panels again.

The room was filled with eerie shadows from the dim candlelight. The men lined up by the table near the wooden box.

One tall man stood behind the box. He lifted the box's lid and spoke with an accent.

He said, "Each man will reach into the box. He will take out one slip of paper."

*That must be Captain Ferrandini,* Patrick thought.

The captain continued, "One slip is marked with a red dot."

Another man asked, "What does the paper with the red dot mean?"

The captain's face twisted into a mean grin. He said, "The man who draws the red dot is the one who will kill President-elect Lincoln!"

Several men said, "Hear! Hear!"

Eugene asked, "How will the plot to kill the president work?"

The captain answered, "Mr. Lincoln will be coming by train to Baltimore and arrive at Calvert Station."

"The Lincoln Special arrives on Saturday," Eugene said. "We can have someone send us a telegram when the train leaves

Harrisburg. Then we will know Lincoln's arrival time."

Several men clapped.

Mr. Hillard said, "Brilliant idea, Mr. Davies. I'll go to Harrisburg."

*Eugene is smart in any century*, Patrick thought.

Luckett said, "I'll go with Mr. Hillard and spy on Mr. Lincoln. We'll return late Friday and be here for Lincoln's ruin."

The men murmured in agreement.

Captain Ferrandini cleared his throat. All eyes turned to him. He said, "Crowds of people will be at Calvert Station to greet him. The police will make a narrow passageway for him from the depot to his carriage. A tunnel, if you will."

The captain took a dagger out of his suit coat pocket. He raised it in the air as if he were going to stab someone.

The evil expression on Captain Ferrandini's face startled Patrick. He shivered.

The captain added, "Mr. Lincoln is destined to die in this tunnel!"

Beth squeezed closer to Patrick. She could now peek between the curtain panels too.

Beth watched as the first man in line reached inside the box. He pulled out a small, white paper. The man put it in his pocket without opening it. Each man did the same. Soon all twenty men had a piece of paper, even Eugene.

Finally Captain Ferrandini drew a slip. Then he replaced the box's lid.

He said, "The day after tomorrow, we will meet at the depot at noon. We will spread out in the crowd. The man with the red dot will attack Mr. Lincoln. No one will know the identity of our hero until that moment. The rest of us will help him escape."

The men moved toward the door in silence.

Soon only Eugene, Hillard, and Ferrandini remained.

Captain Ferrandini said, "Mr. Hillard, come outside with me for a cigar. Then I'll ask Old Newton to drive you home in his buggy."

Hillard and the captain took their hats from a hat rack. They began walking to the main door.

"I'll blow out the candles, lock the garden door, and clean up," Eugene said to Ferrandini.

"Good," Captain Ferrandini said and chuckled. The rebel leader took a cigar out of his pocket. He leaned over and lit the end in one of the burning candles.

Beth heard the front door close behind them.

Eugene came toward the curtains. He moved the fabric aside and opened the glass door. He motioned for Beth and Patrick to step into the garden.

"I'll join you shortly," he said.

Beth felt a chill as she followed Patrick outside. She realized she wasn't wearing a cloak. She wasn't even wearing the same outfit. The Imagination Station had given her new clothes. The pale orange-and-blue plaid dress she now wore wasn't very warm.

Beth heard footsteps.

Patrick whispered, "Shhh." He pulled her behind a large holly bush.

They crouched behind it. One of the pointed leaves pricked Beth's cheek, but she didn't cry out.

Captain Ferrandini and Hillard paused under a large, bare tree.

Ferrandini puffed on his cigar. He leaned

against the tree. Hillard put his hand in his suit jacket pocket.

"Why don't you check your paper?" Ferrandini asked. "I know you're curious."

Hillard reached inside his suit pocket and pulled out his slip of paper. He fiddled with it.

Beth and Patrick couldn't see the paper. But they could see Hillard's frown. They heard him say, "I have a white paper. I won't be the one who will save the South."

Captain Ferrandini laughed. It spilled out of him like smoke from a dragon.

"What's the joke?" Hillard asked. He seemed angry. "Don't you think I'm brave enough?"

Hillard reached inside his suit pocket again. This time he pulled out a pistol. It had a long, metal barrel and a black handle.

Ferrandini pushed the barrel aside. "Put that away until Saturday," he said. "I can see you want to get the job done. I don't care how many

people try to kill the chief traitor. But listen."
The captain leaned toward Hillard and spoke.

The cousins couldn't hear him.

Hillard gave a whoop.

"Eight?" Hillard said. "Eight men drew red dots?"

The captain nodded, then took a draw on his cigar. "Not one," he said, "but *eight* assassins will be waiting for Mr. Lincoln at the Baltimore depot."

Beth gasped.

The men turned. Hillard's pistol turned with him. It was aimed at the holly bush.

# Kate Warne

Patrick heard the rumble of the Imagination Station. It appeared next to a large bush.

*We're saved!* Patrick thought. The car was three giant steps to his left. He knew the men couldn't see it.

*Bang!*

The pistol went off.

Patrick reached to push Beth to the ground. But she was already on her stomach and crawling toward the Imagination Station. He dropped to the ground too. The cousins moved like crabs, sideways, in the dirt. Patrick watched Hillard and Ferrandini's every move.

Hillard fumbled with the gun.

Ferrandini was now at the holly bush. The tall man pushed aside the branches. He said, "They're children!"

Ferrandini pulled out his knife and took off the sheath. "Put away your gun, Hillard," he said.

The captain looked Patrick directly in the eyes. "Who sent you?" the man asked. "Tell me or you'll never talk again!"

"Umm . . . someone from . . . far away," Patrick said, still moving toward the Imagination Station. Out of the corner of his eye, he saw Beth climb into the rumble seat.

"Hurry!" Beth said.

Patrick quickly stood. He yanked open the driver's-side door and dived inside. Ferrandini lunged toward the bush. Patrick turned the wheel and hit the red button on the center of the horn.

*Blatt!*

The windshield spun into a kaleidoscope of color.

Patrick watched, almost dizzied by the flashing colors. Soon it felt as if he were spinning too.

*Oh no!* he thought. *We've left Eugene behind.*

Then everything went black.

Beth suddenly found herself standing in a large room. Grand windows showed the night sky. Six large light fixtures hanging from a paneled ceiling lit the room.

Beth scanned the room. No Imagination Station. No Patrick. But she wasn't alone.

Three women sat on wooden benches around the center of the room. Another woman sat in a rocking chair several yards away.

Beth turned around. Her shoes made a clicking sound on the brown, clay tile. A train schedule for Friday, February 22, 1861 hung next to a large, wooden door with a window above it. The sign on it said *Ladies' Lounge* and *To the PW&B platform.* At the very bottom were the words *Philadelphia, Wilmington, and Baltimore Railroad.*

She didn't know which of the three cities she was in.

*What am I doing here?* she wondered. The Imagination Station had moved her forward by one day. She decided to check for a clue from Eugene. She slid her hand into her dress pocket.

Beth found a slip of paper. *Telegram* was written across the top. Beth knew about telegraph machines from school. People in the 1800s and 1900s used them before telephones were invented. Messages were sent via wires from a machine in one city to a machine in another. Most train stations had one.

The message said:

> OF GREAT IMPORTANCE! IDENTIFY KATE
> WARNE IN THE PHILADELPHIA TRAIN
> STATION'S LADIES' LOUNGE. GIVE HER
> ASSISTANCE. SHE MUST NOT MISS HER
> TRAIN! KEEP HER NAME CONCEALED. E. M.

Beth thought she understood what the telegram meant. The *E. M.* was for Eugene Meltsner.

She needed to find someone named Kate Warne. And she had to do it quickly. But she had to keep the woman's name a secret.

She looked at the four women in the lounge. Two sat together on a bench and chatted.

Beth moved next to a rocking chair near them.

"My train is leaving soon," said a small woman in a dark-blue cloak. "Tomorrow the city is going to be crowded. Mr. Lincoln will be traveling through here." She had dimples even when she didn't smile.

A slender woman in a black cloak sat next to the small woman. She had an honest face capped by brown hair pulled back into a bun. "Mrs. Johnson, I'm surprised you don't want to hear him speak," the second woman said in a Southern drawl.

*That helped,* Beth thought. *The woman in blue isn't Kate Warne.*

"I am not political, Mrs. Cherry," Mrs. Johnson said.

*That was easy too,* Beth thought. She was glad people spoke formally in this century.

Beth looked at the other women in the room.

A gray-haired woman sat and knitted in a rocking chair in the corner. She wore a black dress. Her hat looked like a doily with black lace around the edges.

A cheerful young lady sat on a bench facing away from the knitter. Her curly, black hair was pulled above her alert, brown eyes and smooth, brown skin. She wore a stylish white scarf in the neckline of a black shirt. She also wore a long skirt. Beth wondered about the woman. Perhaps she was a freed slave. Maybe she was Kate Warne.

The woman's eyes met hers. She had a kind smile. Beth walked over to her.

"Hello," Beth said. "My name is Beth."

"How do you do," the woman said. "I am Catherine. How may I be of service to you?"

"I thought you might need *my* assistance," Beth said.

The young woman laughed. "No," she said.

"I work for the railroad. It's my job to help female train travelers. I'm headed to New York in a few minutes."

Beth doubted she was Kate Warne. Beth said, "It was very nice to meet you, Catherine."

The young woman nodded. Beth turned toward the older woman. She had to be Kate Warne. Beth walked over to her.

The woman's knitting needles clicked against each other with each stitch. A string of yarn came out of her bag.

Beth stopped in front of her.

"Hello," Beth said. "My name is Beth. Do you need help?"

The woman stopped knitting. She looked at Beth. "I do," the woman said. "Stretch your hands toward me."

Beth smiled. She lifted her hands with her palms facing each other.

The older woman opened her bag and

pulled out a skein of yellow yarn. She untwisted it and looped it around Beth's upright hands. The woman took one end of it and began rolling the single strand into a ball.

"I was almost done with my roll," the woman said.

Beth's eyebrows drew together. She was helping this woman knit. Beth doubted Eugene had meant this.

"What are you making?" Beth asked politely.

"A baby blanket," the woman said. "My daughter is having another baby."

Beth needed more information. She asked, "Will your new grandchild be named after you?"

"I hope not," she said. "We want it to be a boy."

Beth tried again to find out the woman's first name. "Are any of your grandchildren named after you?" Beth asked.

The woman thought for a moment. "There is little Susie, and my name is Suzanna, so it's close enough."

This was not Kate Warne. Then Beth's eyes grew large. Susie was short for Suzanna.

*Oh no!* Beth thought. *Kate is short for Catherine.*

Beth whipped around to spot Catherine. The young woman had picked up her carpetbag. She was walking toward the lounge door.

Beth had a sinking feeling that Kate Warne might be leaving. She had to get to her before she disappeared completely.

But Beth couldn't leave. Her hands were tied up. The older woman kept rolling the yarn into a larger and larger ball.

Beth glanced toward the door. It closed behind Catherine.

A man's voice boomed from the boarding deck, "All aboard for New York!"

Beth felt trapped. She couldn't do anything without dropping the yarn. And that would be rude.

Finally, Suzanna wound the last strands from Beth's hands.

"Thank you," Suzanna said. She went back to her knitting.

"You're welcome," Beth said. She hoped she wasn't too late. She hurried toward the door. Just then a train whistle tooted. The engine roared to life, and the train rolled out of the station.

*No!* Beth thought. *Kate Warne has left without me!*

# Secret Meetings

Patrick opened his eyes. He was lying on a cream-colored sofa. The material felt silky. He sat up and looked around. The Imagination Station sat in the center of a room with couches, low tables, and armchairs. The machine slowly faded away.

Beth wasn't there.

But Abraham Lincoln was.

The tall man was asleep in a nearby armchair. His black bag sat on the floor near his feet.

"Mr. Lincoln," Patrick said softly. "Hello."
Lincoln opened his eyes.

"I didn't see you come in, Patrick," Lincoln

said. "When did you get to
Harrisburg?" He gave Patrick
a warm smile.

Patrick smiled in return.
"Just now," Patrick said.

"It's a pleasure to have your
company again," Lincoln said. "But I'm sorry
to disappoint you. My sons Willie and Tad are
with Mrs. Lincoln. They're in their rooms."

"I'm sorry I won't get to see them," Patrick
said. "But I came to talk to you."

Patrick looked around the room. He walked
to the large window and closed the thick
drapes. Then he moved toward Mr. Lincoln
and leaned forward.

"There's a plot against your life," Patrick
said.

"Yes," Lincoln said. He calmly folded his hands and rested them in his lap. "I recently received a disturbing letter. It said someone was going to put spiders in my dumplings." The president-elect chuckled. "Would you like to be my food tester to make sure I'm not poisoned?"

*Spiders?* Patrick's stomach churned. He felt his hands turn cold and clammy. "Well . . . if you need me to," he said slowly. He knew it wouldn't be right to say no to the president-elect.

Lincoln laughed louder. "Don't worry," he said. "I'll test my own food. It'll take more than a pie of spiders to stop me."

"Yes, it will," Patrick said. He felt relieved. "But there's more. I have information from Baltimore."

The president-elect sat up straighter. He raised an eyebrow. "What did you learn?" Lincoln said.

The door to the room opened. Seven men

entered. Patrick recognized them. The men had all been passengers on the Lincoln Special and had been allowed to sit in the Lincolns' train car.

The last man to enter the room closed the doors.

A short, barrel-shaped man said, "Good gracious, Patrick. Where did you come from? How did you get past us?"

Lincoln stood and said, "That's no way to greet our friend, Mr. Judd."

Judd scowled behind his gray beard. His dark-blue eyes glared at Patrick. An unlit cigar dangled from his mouth.

Another man with a white beard spoke up. He wore a military uniform with a long coat and lots of buttons down the front. "Why did you call this meeting, Mr. Judd?" he asked.

"Be patient, Colonel Sumner," Judd said. "I'll explain."

Judd moved to the doors and opened them a crack. He peeked outside, then shut them again.

Patrick guessed he was checking to make sure no one outside was listening.

Judd motioned for the men to gather near him.

The group huddled close, even Lincoln.

Patrick squeezed in between Lincoln and the colonel. He looked up at the circle of men with their bushy beards and long sideburns. The expressions of Lincoln's friends were serious. Each man seemed to care deeply for him.

"Rebels in Baltimore are planning mayhem," Judd said.

"May-hem?" Patrick said. "I thought it was February."

All the men laughed, except Lincoln. He laid a hand on Patrick's back. He said, "Mayhem means violent destruction, even unto death. In this case, Mr. Judd seems to think it will be *my* death."

Patrick nodded. Judd was right. But a sliver of fear crept up his back.

Were all these men loyal to Lincoln? He studied each face. What if even one had plotted with Captain Ferrandini?

Beth didn't know what to do. She hadn't followed Catherine, the woman who boarded the train to New York. She wished she could talk to Patrick or Eugene. She checked her pockets again for another clue or a train ticket. But she had nothing besides the first telegram. She plopped down in a rocking chair to think.

The Southern woman in the black cloak

leaned toward her. "Why so down, honey?" Mrs. Cherry asked.

Beth sighed. "I missed my train to New York," she said.

"And that was the last New York train for today," Mrs. Johnson said.

Beth sighed. Catherine was really gone.

"I know how it feels to be stranded," Mrs. Johnson said. "I almost missed a train to my granny's house when I was about eight years old. My mother found me playing on the depot platform. Mama scolded me, 'Sarah May Caufield, pay attention.'"

*Caufield?* Beth thought quickly. *Johnson is this woman's married name. Her maiden name was Caufield. Maybe Warne was Mrs. Cherry's maiden name.*

Beth allowed herself to feel a bit of hope. Perhaps Kate Warne was still in the lounge.

Mrs. Cherry asked, "What will you do now?"

"I don't know," Beth said. "I was supposed to meet someone to get my *tic-KATE*, I mean ticket. I was *warned* not to miss my train."

"Maybe I can be of assistance," Mrs. Cherry said. She stood.

"Have a safe trip, young lady," Mrs. Johnson said.

"Thank you, ma'am," Beth said.

Mrs. Cherry picked up her carpetbag. She headed toward the exit.

Beth hurried ahead and pulled the heavy door open for her.

Mrs. Cherry passed through, and Beth guided the door shut.

The woman faced Beth. Her dark eyes held a

serious expression. She studied Beth's face for a few seconds.

"Who are you?" the woman said. She no longer spoke with a Southern drawl. "And what do you want with *Kate Warne?*"

# The Plan

Patrick finished studying each face. He decided these men could be trusted.

A man with silver hair broke away from the circle of men. Patrick knew him as Mr. Wood.

"How do we know the Baltimore plot is real?" Wood asked. He put his hands in the pockets of his long, navy-blue coat.

Wood turned to the group. "Mr. Lincoln has had a bomb sent to him," Wood said. "Someone tried to derail the train. He's received many threatening letters. But we've been in dozens of cities. He's shaken hands with thousands. And no one has threatened him face-to-face."

Lincoln nodded in agreement. "I don't think the heart of the country is so dark," he said. "The crowds have crushed around me. But no man has done more than squeeze my hand too tightly."

A few of the men chuckled. Patrick laughed too.

"This is a private and serious meeting," Judd said. He glared at Patrick again with his intense blue eyes. He took the unlit cigar out of his mouth. "May we remove the child?"

Patrick looked up at the president-elect.

"Patrick is loyal," Lincoln said. He nodded at Patrick to reassure him. "Continue, Mr. Judd."

Judd cleared his throat. "In Baltimore, the hatred runs deep," he said. "There is a plot to murder the president-elect. I have heard this from two sources: the son of a senator from New York, and Mr. Allan Pinkerton himself."

Lincoln's advisors showed signs of surprise. Eyes widened. Jaws dropped.

Patrick's heart quickened at the mention of Pinkerton's name. The great detective had been in one of the earlier Imagination Station adventures.

"I'll be as safe in Baltimore as anywhere," Lincoln said. "We have two reports. But they could be the same rumor told by two men."

Patrick knew he had to speak. This was why the Imagination Station had brought him here.

"I overheard some men in Baltimore," Patrick said. "There's a plot. The rebels are planning to kill Mr. Lincoln. They plan to strike at the Calvert station."

Judd seemed startled. He pulled on the

strap of his black bowtie to loosen it. "Thank you for taking my side," Judd said to Patrick. "But you are only a child. I believe you're being fanciful."

Mr. Wood shook his head. He said, "I know Patrick to be reliable and responsible. Let the boy tell us what he knows."

The faces of all the men turned toward Patrick.

Patrick took a deep breath. He told the men about the meeting in Baltimore and the box with the paper slips. He described Captain Ferrandini and Mr. Hillard.

Patrick came to the part about the conversation in the small garden. "Then Mr. Hillard showed the captain his paper. I heard the captain say, '*Eight* assassins will be waiting for Mr. Lincoln at the Baltimore depot.'"

"And?" Judd said. "What happened next?"

"Mr. Hillard shot toward the bushes,"

Patrick said. "And . . ." He couldn't tell them about the Imagination Station. He didn't know what to say next.

Mr. Wood whooped and slapped Patrick on the back. "See," he said. "Patrick is willing to take a bullet for Mr. Lincoln!"

Cheers filled the room.

Lincoln sat back down in the armchair. His hands rested on the armrests. "It seems to be true," he said thoughtfully. "I cannot ignore a senator's son, a famous detective, and my friend Patrick."

Colonel Sumner stood next to Lincoln's armchair like a soldier on watch. The colonel said, "I'll get a squad of cavalry, sir. We can cut our way to Washington, DC!"

"Hear, hear!" said a number of voices.

Patrick agreed. An army sounded like a good idea. "Hear, hear!" he said.

"No, no, no!" Judd said. "We can't get the

cavalry together in a few hours. The Lincoln
Special is scheduled to go through Calvert
Station in Baltimore tomorrow afternoon. We
must act tonight."

The room quieted.

"The rebels will not get past
me!" a man said loudly
with a Southern accent.
He was a heavy man
and tall, but not as
tall as Lincoln.
A belt around
his hips held
two pistols in
holsters. "I will walk
by Mr. Lincoln's side
and fight off dozens of
men."

"Mr. Lamon," Judd
said, "we all

know you're ready to fight for Mr. Lincoln.
But Mr. Pinkerton and I have made a more
cunning plan. We will sneak Mr. Lincoln into
Washington tonight."

"A day early?" Wood said.

Colonel Sumner frowned. He said, "Allow
the president to sneak away like a frightened
kitten? No! He'll be laughed at by friend and
foe alike. It will be political death."

Men in the room murmured agreement.

Lincoln stood and straightened his suit
coat. "I've fully thought over the matter,"
Lincoln said. "I may be
called a coward. But if
that's the worst of it, we will
follow Mr. Pinkerton and Mr.
Judd's plan."

Patrick sighed with relief. He didn't want
the president-elect anywhere near Captain
Ferrandini.

Lincoln said, "Now, if you'll excuse me, I want to wash up before we have dinner with Governor Curtin."

The president-elect picked up his bag. He left the room.

Lamon turned to Judd. "Sneaking the president aboard the train will be harder than hiding a giraffe," Lamon said.

Patrick could hear a crowd forming outside. Excited voices carried into the room.

Lamon walked quickly to the door.

The guns on the large man's belt swayed side to side with each step. He closed the door and came back to the center of the room. He motioned for the men to gather close again.

"What is our plan to hide the president, then?" Lamon asked Judd.

"Only one person will go with Mr. Lincoln," Judd said. "The rest of us will ride the Lincoln

Special to Maryland. Everything must seem normal."

"Then the honor and responsibility are mine," Colonel Sumner said. "I am the senior military officer." He pointed to the gold patch on the shoulder of his blue uniform. "I outrank you all. I will be in charge of going with the president to Washington."

Several men nodded in agreement. But Lamon glared at Sumner. The younger man's hand hovered above a pistol.

*Oh no!* Patrick thought. *They're going to fight.*

# Spies

Beth's throat tightened in fear.

"I need to find . . . the person you mentioned," Beth said. "A friend sent me a telegram."

A new train pulled into the station, tooting its whistle twice. The engine hissed. A puff of steam floated across the depot platform.

"I received a telegram earlier today also," Mrs. Cherry said. She seemed as cautious as Beth.

"E. M.?" Beth asked.

Mrs. Cherry nodded. "What is your name?"

"Elisabeth, but Beth for short," Beth said.

Mrs. Cherry seemed satisfied. She reached into her bag for a slip of paper and handed it to Beth.

Beth opened the paper and read the telegram:

OF PARAMOUNT IMPORTANCE! TRUST BETH.
SHE WILL PROVIDE ASSISTANCE ON THE
TRAIN. PINKERTON APPROVES. E. M.

The telegram was definitely from Eugene. There were too many big words for it to be from an imposter.

Mrs. Cherry leaned forward. "Is E. M. why you're looking for Kate Warne?"

Beth nodded.

Masses of people began to get off a train. The baggage car was opened, and railroad workers started to move luggage.

Mrs. Cherry put her hand on Beth's back. She moved her to a dark corner of the train platform. They stood below one of the rectangular windows. The woman smiled and quietly said, "My real name is Kate Warne. Mrs. Cherry is my undercover name."

"A woman detective?" Beth said.

"I am the first," Kate said. "No one will suspect me. My boss is Detective Pinkerton."

Beth smiled, remembering Mr. Pinkerton from their previous adventure. Beth said, "I am honored to meet you."

Kate smiled. "And I, you."

Beth looked around. She said, "What train do we need to catch?"

"We will catch the next train to Baltimore," Kate said. "It doesn't leave until 10:50 p.m."

*That's way past my bedtime,* Beth thought. "What do we do until then?" she said.

"Good detectives must notice details," Kate said. "After I buy your ticket, we'll watch the comings and goings on the platform. Tell me if anyone or anything seems amiss."

Beth nodded. "Amiss for what?" she asked.

Kate studied Beth again.

"A hard task is ahead of us," Kate said. She bent closer to Beth to keep her voice low. "Mr. Pinkerton asked me to smuggle a valuable package out of Philadelphia."

Beth gulped. She wondered if the "package" was President-elect Lincoln. Then she said, "What happens if we're caught?"

"We may not live to tell our side of the story," Kate said.

Judd put a hand on the older man's shoulder. "Colonel," Judd said, "you are well-known as a military threat. Your uniform and long, white beard will alert the reporters. We must keep you far from Mr. Lincoln. Our plan is based on secrecy. Lamon will go as Mr. Lincoln's bodyguard."

Lamon relaxed. Patrick marveled at the man's thick hands. They looked strong enough to snap a brick in half.

"No!" Sumner said. "General Winfield Scott of the United States Army appointed me to protect the president-elect. I will not be removed from my duties by a Southern-born hothead. Even if he is the size of an ox."

Patrick looked at the men's faces. He could tell each one wanted to protect Lincoln. They seemed to love Mr. Lincoln as much as Ferrandini's men hated him.

Judd shook his head, and the group broke up. Some moved toward the door. They left as Lincoln had. But Lamon, Sumner, and Judd remained.

"Pinkerton's plan is made. He will be waiting for Mr. Lincoln in Philadelphia. And one of his people, a woman, will help us," Judd said. He waved his cigar at Sumner.

Then Judd and Lamon left the room together. The military man sat down in a plush armchair. He motioned for Patrick to come close.

"Patrick," he said, "I might not be able to stay with Mr. Lincoln. But *you* can."

"How?" Patrick said.

"A child can always find a way," Sumner

said. "I'm only sixty-four. But these men are treating me as if I'm a doddering old fool."

Patrick thought of the inventor of the Imagination Station, Mr. Whittaker. His friend was about that same age. Old didn't mean someone wasn't clever and capable.

"I'll follow your orders, sir," Patrick said.

Sumner reached into his jacket pocket. He brought out some dollar bills and coins.

"Use this however you need to," the colonel said. He handed Patrick the money.

Patrick pushed the money into his jacket pocket.

Sumner stood and motioned for Patrick to follow him. They left the room.

Men and women in fancy clothing filled the hotel's hallway. They seemed to be trying to get into the nearby dining room. They pushed one another like children in line for candy.

Patrick watched as people parted for the colonel.

Patrick was not so important. He was squished between a woman in a black gown and the wall. He scooted past her. A button from her dress scratched his hand.

Patrick zigged and zagged to the end of the hall. He found a railing and leaned over to breathe fresh air. He was on a second-floor landing looking down into the hotel lobby.

That's when he saw them: Two men in long, black suits pushed their way toward the hotel's front door. Patrick recognized them from Captain Ferrandini's home. One was Mr. Hillard, and the other was Mr. Luckett. They must have taken a train from Baltimore to Harrisburg that morning.

Mr. Hillard looked up.

Patrick locked eyes with him. Then Hillard tapped Luckett's shoulder and said something to him. Luckett glanced up at Patrick too.

Patrick backed away too late. Now two men could recognize him.

The men quickly went out the front door.

*Are they spying?* Patrick wondered. *Or are they here to kill Mr. Lincoln?*

# The Crowds

Patrick moved away from the railing. He saw the colonel's white hair. The old man was moving toward the dining room.

"Colonel Sumner!" Patrick called.

The old man didn't turn.

More people entered the hallway.

"Excuse me," Patrick said several times. But no one paid attention to him. Finally he dropped down to his knees and crawled. He moved between and around the legs of people. One woman stepped on his hand.

"Ow!" he said.

"What are you doing down there?" she said and lifted her foot.

Finally Patrick reached Sumner.

Patrick tugged on the colonel's pant leg.

The colonel glanced down. He looked surprised.

"I told you a child can go where a grownup can't," Sumner said. He smiled. The colonel offered Patrick his hand.

Patrick clasped the old man's hand, and the colonel pulled him upright.

"I saw them!" Patrick said. "Two of the Baltimore men plotting Mr. Lincoln's—"

Sumner clamped a hand over Patrick's mouth. The colonel's skin smelled like tobacco and soap.

"Spies lurk everywhere," the old man said in a low voice.

Patrick nodded. Sumner removed his hand.

"Show me where they went," the colonel said quietly.

Patrick led the colonel away from the dining room. They walked down the stairs and out the front door.

A cold gust blew across the hotel steps. Patrick shivered.

Patrick scanned the area. Carriages and horses came and went on the dirt street. A man in a black suit and top hat stepped down from a carriage. A laughing woman and two young men hailed another.

Only one carriage stood still. It waited across the street from the Jones House hotel. The driver stood next to it. He was patting the nose of a white horse.

"Do you see the villains?" Sumner asked.

Patrick shook his head. "They're gone," he said. Patrick pointed across the street. "That carriage hasn't moved."

"There's a reason for that," Sumner said. He leaned closer to Patrick and said softly, "That carriage will take Mr. Lincoln to the train station. I recognize the driver."

Patrick scanned the crowd one last time. People watched from windows and waited on the hotel steps. "Mr. Hillard and Mr. Luckett may be watching. They might be able to recognize the driver too," Patrick said.

The colonel's face turned as white as his beard. "Yes," he said. "That's a military tactic: 'Know your enemy.'"

Suddenly Patrick knew what he had to do.

Kate and Beth walked along the PW&B depot's platform in Philadelphia. A train

from Harrisburg arrived. Beth tried to
study each passenger. But she didn't see
everyone. Some left for trains.
Others arrived and were in the
shadows.

Everyone seemed ordinary
to Beth. But so had the men
in Ferrandini's home.

The gas lamps glowed
weakly.

Kate put down her
carpetbag. She pulled out a
round watch that had been
tucked into her belt. The
watch was attached to a
chain.

Kate said, "We can board
our train now."

"Which train is ours?" Beth said.

Kate pointed to one that was just ahead of the train from Harrisburg. "It won't leave for an hour. But we can board. Then we can reserve spots in the front. That way the package won't have to pass through the train cars. Fewer people will see it."

Beth understood now. Lincoln *was* the "package." He would arrive after everyone else was on board. He would sit near the train car door and be the first person off. It seemed like a good plan.

Just then two men in dark suits got off the Harrisburg train. They walked quickly and seemed confident. One of them lifted his hat when he saw Kate.

Beth muffled a gasp by pretending to sneeze. "Ha-choo!" she said.

"What's wrong?" Kate asked.

The men approached the train to Baltimore and began talking to the conductor.

Beth leaned close to Kate. "I saw those men in Baltimore," Beth said. "They want Mr. Lincoln dead." Beth took a deep breath to steady herself. "The taller one has a pistol, and he's prepared to use it."

# Preparing to Travel

Sumner and Patrick walked across the street to the carriage.

The driver gave a slight bow to Sumner. "How may I serve you?" the driver asked the colonel.

"My young friend would like to sit inside the carriage," Sumner said. "He'll wait for the rest of our party."

The colonel gave the driver a coin. The driver quickly opened the carriage door. Patrick climbed inside the dark chamber.

The carriage blocked the wind. But Patrick still shivered. The windows were covered with gold-and-black curtains, so no light came inside.

A brown blanket was on one bench. Patrick recognized it from the Lincoln Special. It belonged to the president-elect.

The colonel stood at the door. He said, "Go ahead and use the blanket. You've got a long wait."

Patrick pulled the blanket over his legs.

Then the colonel said, "I'm leaving to talk some sense into Mr. Lincoln. I should ride with him, not Mr. Lamon." The colonel closed the door.

"Goodbye, sir," Patrick said.

Patrick leaned against the side of the carriage. He pushed back the curtains and looked outside.

He searched for top hats in the crowd.

He hoped to see Hillard's or Luckett's face beneath them.

Finally, Patrick felt the carriage move. The horses brought the carriage to the side of the hotel. He let the curtains fall. The carriage door swung open.

Lamon climbed inside. He sat in the seat next to Patrick. His jacket fell open. Patrick saw two large pistols, a bowie knife, and a leather-covered baton. He also saw that Lamon's right-hand fist clutched a pair of brass knuckles. The big man was ready to fight for Lincoln.

Lamon gave Patrick a nod in greeting.

Patrick nodded back.

Next a man in a soft-
brimmed fabric hat and
a brown overcoat climbed
inside. He sat on the seat
across from Patrick. The tall man dropped a
black oilskin bag on the floor.

Patrick recognized the bag.

The man gave a grim smile. "Hello, Patrick,"
Lincoln said. "I was hoping you'd be here.

 I need someone to watch
my bag."

"Yes, sir!" Patrick said.

Sumner, standing tall
and dignified, waited next
to the carriage. It seemed as if he wanted to
board.

Judd suddenly pushed the colonel aside.
He poked his head through the carriage

door. The unlit cigar was thrust into the side of his mouth. "No one must recognize the president," Judd said. "Godspeed. I'll telegraph Pinkerton to let him know you've left." Judd stepped back, keeping the colonel from getting on.

Lamon pulled the door shut.

Patrick heard the driver snap the horses' reins. The carriage jerked forward.

Patrick pulled aside the curtain. He peered out. Judd looked pleased. But Sumner had a fist raised in the air.

Lamon said, "Close the curtains, boy. We don't want anyone seeing the president."

Patrick closed the curtains. He wished the colonel had been able to come.

Patrick glanced at Lincoln. The president-elect's kind eyes seemed to understand.

"Patrick, why do you want to look outside?" Lincoln asked.

"I can recognize the men from Baltimore who vowed to kill you," Patrick said. "I saw two of them leaving the hotel earlier."

Lamon sighed. He reached across Patrick and jerked the curtains aside.

"Then start watching," the big man said. "We won't be safe until we're in Washington."

The conductor stood near the train car steps. Beth watched as he punched Luckett's and Hillard's tickets. They boarded the train to Baltimore.

Kate stood up straight. "Did the men recognize you?" she asked Beth.

"No," Beth said. "At Ferrandini's garden they saw only my cousin clearly."

Kate lifted Beth's chin and looked her in the eyes. She said, "You'll make a great detective one day."

Beth felt proud. "What should I do?" she said.

"Come with me," Kate said. She picked up her carpetbag. "Pretend you're my niece Ruby Cherry. The Cherry family is rich and comes from the Deep South. You'll have to speak with an accent."

The conductor approached them. "Hello," he said. "I'm Conductor Litzenberg."

"Hello," Beth said in a slow Southern drawl. Her *O* lasted nearly three syllables. "I'm Ruby." She motioned toward Kate. "And this is Mrs. Cherry, my aunt."

"I'll need to see your tickets, please," Conductor Litzenberg said.

Kate handed him their tickets.

He punched the tickets and handed them back.

Kate said, "My dear relative is an invalid. He's coming late with his caretaker." She was using her Southern drawl again. "May I please reserve the front four berths?"

"No reservations," Litzenberg said. "It's first come, first served. Besides, those berths have already been claimed by others."

Kate's expression fell. She looked crushed. "Please then," Kate said, "may we have the last four berths?"

"That would be hard on your relation, Mrs. Cherry," the conductor said. "He'd have to walk all the way down the aisle. It's a fair distance."

*Surely the spies will see Lincoln. He can't enter from the front!* Beth thought.

Kate was silent for a moment.

Beth said, "May we please enter from the back door? Then our dear relative won't have to walk so far."

Conductor Litzenberg frowned. "No," he said hastily, "the back door is always locked."

He shoved his hands into his pockets. "It's against the rules to unlock it. I'm the only railroad employee on this car. I can't watch two entrances. Someone could sneak on."

*That's exactly what we want to do*, Beth thought. *Sneak Lincoln on board.*

"Then would you help us carry my dear relation?" Kate asked. "He's not heavy." Her voice was as sweet as honey.

The conductor twitched his moustache. He didn't seem to like that idea.

"You seem like an honest lady," Conductor Litzenberg said. "I'll unlock the back door. But I don't want to get in trouble. Please don't let any other passengers see your relative boarding."

*No problem*, Beth thought.

"Thank you," Beth said.

Kate echoed Beth's words. Then she said, "This way, child."

"Ruby" and "Mrs. Cherry" walked through each train car.

"Where are the seats?" Beth whispered to Kate.

"It's a sleeper car, and the seats have been folded down," Kate said. "Behind each curtain is a berth with an upper bed and a lower bed."

Finally they reached the last train car. Rows of curtained compartments were on either side of the center aisle.

In the last car, two gentlemen had just claimed two berths across the aisle from each other. They weren't the first set of berths in the last car but the second. Beth recognized the spies Luckett and Hillard.

Kate passed them. She went to the four berths at the end of the train car. A door was at the back of it.

Beth walked past Luckett and Hillard

slowly. She saw the curtains of their berths had been pulled back a bit. Unblinking green eyes were watching her.

# Philadelphia

The carriage stopped. The three of them—
Patrick, Lincoln, and Lamon—hurried toward
Engine 161 at the Harrisburg depot.

"The train looks funny," Patrick said. It
had only one passenger car attached to the
engine.

"Yes," Lamon said. "And we are the only
passengers for the next 100 miles."

"All the way to Philadelphia," Lincoln said.

"Not Washington?" Patrick said.

"No train goes straight from here to Washington," Lincoln said. "We must stop briefly in Philadelphia and then in Baltimore."

No passersby recognized Mr. Lincoln. Patrick knew why. Lincoln wore a different-shaped hat. And his brown shawl was draped over it to cover his craggy features. Lincoln stooped when he walked to appear shorter. He looked nothing like the confident, tall man who had been elected president of the United States.

The disguise should have comforted Patrick. But it only made him worry.

He wondered, *What if Ferrandini's men are wearing disguises too? Will I be able to spot them?*

Only the engineer and his fireman approached the president-elect. The railroad workers quickly ushered them on board the train. Patrick settled in a seat next to Lincoln and sat quietly.

No lights were allowed on. Soon the train sped along.

Patrick didn't speak.

Neither did the men.

There was nothing to do. But Patrick couldn't sleep.

No one else did either.

The train stopped every hour at small stations along the way to fill up with water.

They arrived in Philadelphia four hours after leaving Harrisburg.

Patrick followed Lamon and Lincoln off the train. He scanned the dozen or so people at the depot loading area.

*Those two aren't Ferrandini's men,* he thought. *That one isn't Luckett either. And that tall one isn't Hillard.*

In a dark corner of the depot stood an

enclosed carriage. A man in a black coat was standing near it in the shadows. He was stocky and wore a bowler hat.

The man walked toward them.

Lamon pulled a pistol out of its holster. He gripped Patrick's forearm with the other hand.

"Is that one of the thugs?" he said. "Just say the word and I'll make sure he doesn't get near Mr. Lincoln."

Patrick's heart leaped. He recognized the man's face.

"No!" Patrick said. "That's Allan Pinkerton."

Patrick had met the great detective on

another adventure in 1874. Pinkerton didn't recognize Patrick because that was thirteen years in the future.

"Gentlemen," Pinkerton said. "Allan Pinkerton at your service."

Lamon and Lincoln exchanged greetings with the detective.

"Mr. Judd said you'd meet us here," Lincoln said. "Thank you."

Pinkerton motioned to Patrick and said, "I wasn't aware that William Lincoln was coming."

Lincoln said, "This young lad isn't my son. His name is Patrick. He was in Baltimore and knows the faces of those who wish me ill."

"My pleasure to meet you," Pinkerton said. "My operative Mr. Harry Davies sent me a telegram about you. Mr. Judd did too."

Patrick was glad to know Eugene had sent a telegram. That meant his friend was probably all right. Patrick offered his hand to the detective. "I know Mr. Davies as E. M.," Patrick said.

Pinkerton shook Patrick's hand. "Everything has gone according to my plan," the detective said. "We'll have you safely in Washington by morning. When the assassins wait for you at Calvert Station tomorrow morning, you won't be there."

"Why are we taking a carriage?" Lamon asked. "I thought we were going by train to Baltimore."

"Our train leaves from a station south of here," Pinkerton said. "We must keep Mr. Lincoln hidden until then."

"We can ask the driver to drive slowly," Patrick said.

Pinkerton stroked his thick moustache. "No," Pinkerton said. "We must not alert the driver to anything odd. He's not one of us."

Patrick felt proud to be part of the "us." He couldn't believe he was helping to save President-elect Lincoln's life.

"Perhaps Patrick can search for his *friends*," Lincoln said. All the men turned to look at him.

Patrick said. "I don't have any friends in Philadelphia. But I can look for Mr. Luckett and Mr. Hillard. They were going back to Baltimore. They'll have to come through Philadelphia, right?"

But you have one friend, according to E. M.," Pinkerton said. "Her name starts with the letter B. But you'll have to look carefully, and that means going slowly." He winked at Patrick.

*Beth!* Patrick thought.

"Is this friend near?" Patrick asked the detective.

Pinkerton nodded. "She's in the city," he

said. "You'll see her before the night is over."
The group walked closer to the carriage.

Pinkerton spoke to the carriage driver.
"This lad wants to find his friends," he said.
"Do exactly as he says. Start by going three
blocks north to Vine Street, then go east to
Seventeenth." Pinkerton gave the driver a gold
coin.

"Yes, sir!" the driver said.

Patrick climbed up on the carriage bench
and sat beside the driver.

The night was chilly. The driver opened his
blanket and covered Patrick's legs. That was
much warmer. Then the driver flicked a thin
whip, and the three horses trotted off.

The wooden carriage wheels bumped over
the red cobblestones. The carriage vibrated.

They passed large homes. Patrick didn't see
Beth.

"Maybe over there," Patrick said. The driver turned the carriage.

They passed tall buildings with many windows.

Patrick shook his head. He said, "Let's go that way."

Patrick saw a group of people. He asked the driver to slow down.

He didn't see Beth or Ferrandini's men. They turned one way and then another. Still he didn't recognize anyone.

Someone from inside the carriage thumped on the carriage roof. The driver stopped.

Pinkerton got out. "We can't look any longer," he said. "We need to go to the PW&B station."

"Very good, sir," the driver said.

Patrick was disappointed. But he climbed down.

Pinkerton held the carriage door open.

Patrick saw a brown package the size of a large dictionary under one of the seats. Fear gripped him.

"Mr. Pinkerton," Patrick said in a low voice, "I think I see a bomb."

# The Arrangements

The green-eyed Hillard closed the curtains. She hurried past him to the back of the train car.

"I can lie down in one of these beds," Beth said, "and save the one above me."

"I can take another," Kate said, "and save the berth above me too. I'll put my carpetbag on it. But we need two more."

Beth looked around. She saw a thin, linen drape pulled to one side. A short, fancy rope held it in place.

"This should help," Beth said. She untied the rope. The linen drape opened and blocked the aisle. It separated the back four sets of berths from the rest of the train car.

Ferrandini's men were nearby. But now they would not be able to see Lincoln arrive through the back door.

"Good idea," Kate said.

An older woman with a green scarf peeked around the drape.

"Are these berths open?" she asked. "I like to ride near the back. You can't hear the boilers roar."

"No," Kate said. "I'm sorry. They're taken."

"Very well," the woman said. She dropped the curtain.

Beth turned to ask Kate a question. But before she could, the drape was pulled aside again. This time Luckett peeked in. "Are these taken?" he asked. "I'd like to move here."

Beth's throat tightened. They had to keep
this assassin from entering. But how?

Pinkerton smiled and climbed into the
carriage. His foot tapped the package.

"It's safe enough," Pinkerton said. "I put it
there."

Patrick felt relieved. He
climbed inside the carriage
and sat next to Lincoln.

Pinkerton shut the door.

"We're almost there," Pinkerton said. "We'll
have to be even more careful. We will be
boarding a public train."

Lamon reached inside his coat. He took out
one of his revolvers and his bowie knife.

"You should probably have these," Lamon
said. He offered the weapons to Lincoln.

"No!" Pinkerton said. He pushed the

weapons back toward Lamon. "It's a disgrace for the president to defend himself. The papers will say he entered Washington armed."

"He needs to protect himself," Lamon said. "In Baltimore there are some fifteen thousand who have vowed Mr. Lincoln shall not pass."

Patrick turned cold inside. He'd been worried about only eight.

"I understand your concerns, Mr. Lamon," Lincoln said. "But I trust Mr. Pinkerton. His plan will work."

"And what if it doesn't?" Lamon said.

"I am not afraid," Lincoln said.

Patrick was quiet as the carriage headed toward the PW&B train station. So were the others. Ferrandini's men would have guns and knives. Lincoln planned to meet them without any weapons. Lincoln wasn't afraid, but Patrick was scared for him.

● ● ●

Luckett continued to stare at them. Beth looked to Kate for help.

Kate spoke with a sweet Southern drawl. "They are taken, sir," she said. "My sick relation and his caretakers have been delayed. Didn't I notice you and your friend in the front two berths?"

Beth saw a tall, thin man behind him. It was Hillard. He grinned pleasantly and then said, "We were just making sure there weren't better berths. But I would never displace a lady."

There was an awkward silence.

Beth guessed they wanted to check all the berths. Were they suspicious? Were they already looking for Mr. Lincoln?

"Is your relation contagious?" Luckett asked.

Beth turned to Kate. "Does yellow fever spread easily?" she asked.

Luckett looked pale. He dropped the curtain. He said from the other side of it, "I think our berths up front are fine."

Hillard said, "Good evening, ladies."

"Good night," Kate said.

Beth put her hand over her mouth. She kept a giggle from coming out.

Maybe Luckett was willing to die to save the South. But he wasn't ready to catch yellow fever!

Beth checked the back door to make sure Conductor Litzenberg had unlocked it. The knob turned easily.

She stepped outside. She had been on this type of platform before. She remembered

standing alongside Lincoln as he waved to
crowds of admirers. But that had been on the
Lincoln Special. And Patrick had been with
her. She wondered where he was.

Kate joined her on the platform. "Here,"
the detective said. "Take this to keep warm."
Kate wrapped her black cloak around Beth's
shoulders.

"I'm going back inside to make sure no one
takes our berths," Kate said. She looked at the
watch on her waist chain. "You'll see a group
of men, at least three. Wave them over here.
Be sure to—"

"Tell them about Hillard and Luckett," Beth
said.

Beth heard a whistle. That meant the train
would leave in a few minutes. She thought,
*The package had better arrive soon!*

# The Package

Patrick slouched against the inside of the carriage to rest. But it was bouncing too much.

Pinkerton cleared his throat. "I have another task for you, Patrick," he said.

"Leave the boy alone," Lamon said. "I can do it."

Lincoln chuckled. Mr. Pinkerton frowned.

"Thank you for volunteering, Mr. Lamon," Pinkerton said. "But you need to stay with

President Lincoln." Pinkerton pulled out the box from under his seat.

It was covered in brown paper and had twine wrapped around it.

Pinkerton said, "Patrick, when we get to the train, I want you to go to the front of it. Give this package to the engineer."

Patrick sat up straighter. He was glad to help Lincoln.

Lamon touched the package. He said, "What's in it?"

"Scrap paper," Pinkerton said.

Lamon shook his head. He said, "Why

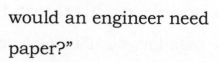

would an engineer need paper?"

Patrick laughed. "No one needs it," he said. "Mr. Lincoln is the real package. This package is a decoy."

Pinkerton nodded. He said, "Give it to

the engineer only after Mr. Lincoln is on the
train."

"Are you leaving me here, then?" Patrick
asked. He looked out the window for the
Imagination Station. It wasn't there.

"No, no," Pinkerton said. "Board the train
after the package is delivered. You'll be looking
for another agent. Her name is Mrs. Cherry.
She'll have your ticket."

The carriage stopped.
Pinkerton opened the door.

Patrick picked up the
package and put it in the
black oilskin bag. Then he
slipped out of the carriage quickly. The driver
didn't even see him leave. The night covered
him like a cape.

Patrick hurried inside the depot. Gas lamps
lit the way with fan-shaped flames. A family
sat on the benches in the large room.

A ticket counter was along one wall. Patrick saw a door to a ladies' lounge and a door to a men's lounge.

Patrick reached the train platform. It was much darker there. It took his eyes a few seconds to adjust.

Patrick held the bag tightly. He didn't want anyone to see him.

Patrick studied the tracks. Only one engine was spouting steam.

*Is that the right train?* Patrick wondered. He couldn't be wrong. Lincoln's life might depend on it.

● ● ●

Beth stood on the train car platform. Cold air stung her cheeks. She snuggled deeper into Kate's black cloak.

Passengers stepped onto the depot platform.

Beth scanned the area. She saw no one she recognized.

Then three people exited the depot. They walked toward the train. Beth strained her eyes.

A brown shawl covered one man's head. He leaned heavily on a stout man with a bowler hat. A third large man in a black suit walked behind them.

They had to be the group she was looking for. Beth needed to get their attention so they didn't board the front of the train.

Beth hurried to the bottom step of the platform. She held the railing and leaned forward, waving her arm.

The three people kept walking toward the train. They didn't see her.

*What can I do?* she thought. She looked down. It was cold, but Kate's black cloak was keeping her warm.

*That's it!* she thought. The night was dark.

So was the cloak. The men hadn't seen her waving.

Beth quickly took off the cloak, draping it over one arm. They should notice her light-colored dress. She started waving again.

Suddenly the three men stopped. They turned and started walking toward her.

Beth backed up when they got to the train car platform.

The man with the shawl over his head placed his foot on the first step. He wore a soft-brimmed brown hat. He looked at her.

"Mr. Lincoln," she said.

Lincoln gave her a slow smile. "It's my friend Beth," he said.

The man in the bowler hat said, "Good evening. My name is Mr. Pinkerton."

"Hello," she said.

Mr. Pinkerton stepped onto the platform.
The third man was one of Lincoln's friends.
She recognized him as a passenger on the
Lincoln Special.

"Hurry," Lamon said. "Let's move away from
prying eyes."

"Mrs. Cherry and I saved you berths at
the back of the train," Beth said. She put her
hand on the door handle and opened the door.

"Very good," Pinkerton said. He pushed
inside. Then he turned to ask Beth, "What's
that curtain?"

"The only thing separating you from
Ferrandini's men," she said.

Patrick ran toward the front of the train
the moment Lincoln stepped onto the back.
Steam billowed from the engine.

"Hello there!" he said. "Hello!"

The engineer looked out an open window. He was wearing a blue baseball-style cap. He wore overalls and a buttoned-up shirt.

The engineer leaned sideways out of the train. "Do you have the package?" he said.

"Here," Patrick said. He took the box out of the oilskin bag. He held it up to the engineer. "Please get it to Baltimore as quick as you can."

The engineer took the package. "Thanks!" he said. He pulled a lever, and the train began to roll.

Patrick watched the baggage car pass. Then he jumped onto the steps of the first passenger car.

The train gave a whistle and moved faster.

Patrick had made it on board. But more importantly, so had Mr. Lincoln.

# A Train Ride

Lincoln quickly hid inside a berth and lay on the top bunk. Lamon climbed onto the bed below him, one pistol drawn. He was ready to stop anyone who wanted to harm the president-elect.

The train sped away from Philadelphia, its wheels clacking on the tracks. Beth leaned against a berth to steady herself from the sudden movement. Then she handed the cloak to Kate. "Thank you for letting me use it," Beth said.

"I'm glad it kept you warm," Kate said. "And I'm grateful for your help."

Pinkerton said, "Beth helped you, and Patrick helped me."

"You've seen Patrick?" Beth said. She grinned. "Where is he?"

Lincoln's voice came from behind the curtain of his berth. "He traveled here with us," he said.

"A stand-up fellow, he is," Lamon said.

"Patrick just delivered a package to the engineer," Pinkerton said. "He will find us soon."

"Oh, no!" Beth said. She pointed to the curtain. She whispered, "*They* will recognize Patrick. I need to warn him."

"Hurry," Kate said.

Beth moved toward the curtain.

She heard the hum of the Imagination
Station.

She peeked around the curtain.

The Imagination Station gradually
appeared in the middle of the train car aisle.
It was on the other side of Ferrandini's men.
In some mysterious way, the car fit in the
small space.

"We may not be able to come back here,"
Beth said to Kate and Pinkerton. "It will
attract attention."

"Then good-bye," Pinkerton said. "And
thank you." He doffed his hat to her.

Kate waved good-bye.

Lincoln stuck the soft-brimmed brown
hat between the curtains and waved with it.
Lincoln said, "I hope we meet again."

"Me too," Beth said.

Beth pulled the linen curtain open. Then
she closed it behind her. She heard snores

from the berths of the spies and moved toward the Imagination Station.

Patrick made his way toward the back of the train. He opened the door of the last car. The Imagination Station was in the aisle.

Eugene stepped out of the machine and smoothed the wrinkles from his black suit. On top of his reddish-brown hair was a stovepipe hat. "Greetings," he said.

"Eugene!" Patrick said.

"Patrick!" It was Beth's voice. He turned toward her. She was sitting in the rumble seat.

Beth said, "Eugene has figured something out."

"So have I," Patrick said. He climbed into the passenger seat. "It's time to go home."

Eugene shook his head slowly. "Not yet,"

he said. "Mr. Whitaker and I have some computations to do. Only then can I be my correct age when we return to Whit's End."

"I don't understand," Patrick said.

"All three of us need to take one more trip back to Baltimore," Eugene said. "Mr. Whittaker will then proceed to fix the code in the machine's computer. Hopefully, I'll be my correct age when we arrive back at Whit's End."

Beth said, "What are we waiting for?"

"You," Eugene said.

"Let's go," Patrick said.

"I'm in," Beth said. "Where are we going?"

Eugene shook his head. "I don't know. Wherever the Imagination Station needs to take us to fix the time line."

Eugene sat behind the wheel of the Model T. His tall hat hit the car's roof. He took it off and put it on the seat. He put on old-fashioned, leather-trimmed goggles.

Beth giggled.

"You look like a bug," Patrick said.

"Laugh not" Eugene said. "Mr. Tesla gave me these driving goggles. In 1921, these were the rage in fashion."

"Is that where you've been?" Patrick asked.

"Among other places," Eugene said.

Patrick set the black bag on the floor. He picked up the hat that was on the seat and put it on.

"You look dignified in that hat," Beth said. "And smarter."

Eugene took hold of the steering wheel and turned it. He slammed his palm on the red button.

*Blatt!*

# *Back to Baltimore*

The spinning dots before Patrick's eyes
suddenly formed into the shapes of people. He
got out of the Imagination Station. It faded.

He and Beth were standing on a road
jammed with people. They were coming into
the city. Carriages rolled past slowly on the
cobblestone streets. Men, women, and children
jostled one another.

Patrick heard people talking about Mr.
Lincoln. Not all of them were happy he was
the newly elected president.

"Let's head toward that tall building,"
Beth said. She was carrying the black bag.
"It's where everyone seems
to be going." She pointed
to a structure with two
towers and keyhole-shaped
windows.

They neared the building.
A train pulled in alongside it. Black smoke
poured out of its fat smokestack.

"This is it!" Beth said. "The sign says it's
Calvert Station."

The station was a hive of excitement.
Railroad employees shepherded people to their
trains. Others called for more water for the
engines.

A series of bell rings sounded from a nearby
building. They rang ten times.

"We have two hours before Mr. Lincoln is to
arrive," Patrick said.

"Maybe we have time to warn him or Mr. Pinkerton," Beth said. "We can send a telegram."

"Hurry," Patrick said. "I'll send a telegram to Colonel Sumner. He'll know what to do. Let's go inside."

The cousins made their way to a wooden counter. There was no line. A sign above it said *Telegraph Office*. A young woman wearing a green visor asked, "How may I help you, dearies?" She smiled sweetly.

Patrick took out one of the silver dollars Sumner had given him. He plunked it down on the counter.

"I'd like to send a telegram," Patrick said.

"Where to?" the woman asked.

"The Jones House hotel in Harrisburg, Pennsylvania," Patrick said.

The woman's smile turned upside

down. "I'm sorry," she said. "The lines to Pennsylvania aren't working."

Patrick glanced at Beth. She seemed pale, and she was biting her lower lip.

"It's the strangest thing," the woman said. "There was no bad weather last night along that telegraph route. It's almost as if someone damaged them on purpose."

"Thank you," Patrick said. He picked up his silver dollar.

The cousins moved outside to the train station steps.

"Why would Ferrandini's men cut the lines?" Beth asked. "You'd think his spies would need to telegraph when Mr. Lincoln left Harrisburg."

"I think Mr. Pinkerton had them cut," Patrick said. "Maybe he didn't want anyone to telegraph that the president had left early."

"I hope so," Beth said.

Someone bumped into Patrick. Eugene's top hat tumbled off his head. He quickly picked it up.

The crowd had formed what looked like a tunnel of people. Some of them looked angry. Policemen held back the crowds on each side.

Patrick pointed toward one end of the tunnel. "Let's go down there," he said. "Away from the building."

"Okay," she said.

Patrick pushed past a couple in matching gray cloaks and then went between two tall men in top hats.

"Stop," one of the men said. He had an accent. Patrick looked up. It was Captain Ferrandini. Beside him was Hillard.

Patrick didn't stop. He dove into the crowd. He went through people so quickly he didn't even see those he passed. But he felt a scratchy wool coat brush against his face.

"Stop that boy!" Hillard said. "He's a pickpocket!"

*The liar*, Patrick thought as he ran. Soon he had put distance between himself and the Baltimore plotters. They couldn't get through the crowd as easily.

Patrick was out of breath by the time he reached the end of the police-controlled tunnel.

Beth wasn't far behind.

"I saw Ferrandini," Patrick said. "And he saw me."

Beth tilted her head. Her eyebrows drew together. "We did keep Mr. Lincoln from coming here. Didn't we?" she asked. "He did get safely to Washington last night?"

"I don't know," Patrick said. "The Imagination Station had to change things to get Eugene back to the correct age. What if our trip has been erased? What if Mr.

Lincoln is still on the Lincoln Special this morning?"

Beth shook her head. She didn't want to believe it could be true. Lincoln had traveled to Washington the previous night. But Ferrandini's men were in the crowd. People were in Baltimore to see the newly elected president. At least eight of them had plans to kill Lincoln.

"What are we going to do?" Patrick said. "If we get too close, Ferrandini or Hillard will grab us."

"You kids," said a loud voice. "This mob is no place for kids. Go home."

Beth looked up. A carriage driver was speaking to them. He was a few yards away. People surrounded his black buggy and horse. He was stuck too.

The man was tall and lean, and he sat up straight as a flagpole. His black cloak covered him. He had dark skin and handsome, brown eyes. His curly, gray hair made him seem regal.

Beth poked Patrick's arm. She said, "Let's ask to sit with him. Maybe we can see more from there."

The bells rang again.

The cousins pushed through the crowd to the small carriage.

"We can't see our parents in this crowd," Patrick said to explain. And he really couldn't see his parents. "May we sit with you?"

"Might as well," the driver said. "I won't be able to pick up more fares in this mob. People won't let my horse, Tim, through."

"My name is Patrick, and this is my cousin Beth," Patrick said. He climbed into the buggy. Beth patted Tim's nose. Then she climbed up and sat beside Patrick.

"It's nice to meet you," the man said. "My name is Old Newton. I've been bringing people here all morning. Everyone wants to see Mr. Lincoln."

Beth set Lincoln's bag on Patrick's lap. She sat on the buggy seat and studied the crowd.

"Everyone is pushing," Patrick said. "They need police to keep a narrow pathway cleared."

"I hope Mr. Lincoln has guards when he gets off the train," Old Newton said.

*Mr. Lamon is powerful,* Beth thought. *But if Mr. Lincoln is on that train, he'll need an army to protect him.*

# Old Newton

Patrick nudged Beth. He pointed toward the Calvert Station platform.

The two killers had worked their way to the front. Hillard and Captain Ferrandini were mingling with the police.

The police seemed to be giving them spots near the depot opening. Then Luckett appeared. Ferrandini gave his place to him. Next, Hillard gave his place to another man from the Baltimore meeting.

"It's good to see some concerned citizens helping our police," Old Newton said.

"They're not good citizens," Beth said. She and Patrick exchanged a glance. The men from the Baltimore meeting would be close enough to hurt Lincoln.

Patrick looked toward the Baltimore men again. Ferrandini was staring straight at him. The man's dark eyes seemed to glow with hatred. He moved a hand inside his coat.

*Does he have a weapon?* Patrick wondered.

"Quick," Patrick said to Beth. "Hide me. Captain Ferrandini can recognize me. He saw me in the garden!"

Beth sat up straight in the carriage. Patrick sat behind her and ducked. His hat fell off. He peeked around the carriage bench to study his enemy.

Ferrandini was now shaking Hillard's

shoulder. The captain motioned toward the carriage with wild arm movements.

"It's too late," Beth said. "They saw you." Beth picked up the black hat that had fallen off Patrick's head.

The men started to push through the crowd toward the cousins.

Patrick looked around the area. There was nowhere to go. They were stuck in the mass of people.

Ferrandini and Hillard came close to the carriage. Ferrandini spit on the ground. "Who sent you to spy on us?" he said.

Old Newton raised his horsewhip. "Move on," he said to the captain. "I already have passengers. There's no room for more."

Hillard scowled. He eyed Old Newton.

"You can't stop us anyway," Ferrandini said to the cousins. "Today the South will be saved!"

Ferrandini grabbed a bowie knife at his waist.

Patrick gasped.

Old Newton's whip snapped. The knife fell. It hit the cobblestones with a clatter.

Ferrandini began to bend down. It seemed he wanted to pick up the blade. But he eyed Old Newton's whip.

Ferrandini said, "We don't want any trouble with you, old man."

"I don't want any trouble for anyone," Old Newton said. "Be off." He snapped his whip again.

Quick as a snake, Ferrandini went down on one knee and picked up his knife. Then he and Hillard merged into the crowd.

"They don't like a fair fight," Patrick said. "They were afraid of your whip."

"I'm pretty good with it," Old Newton said. He chuckled and put the whip down next to him.

The crowd drew tighter around the carriage. The police were pushing hard against the crowd to keep a narrow tunnel free for Lincoln.

An angry group chanted, "Go back home, Mr. Lincoln! Go home!"

Someone in the crowd threw a rock. It whizzed past Patrick and dinged a woman in the head.

She shrieked. And then the chaos began.

Beth saw a fistfight break out between two men wearing top hats. One ended up with a fat lip. The other received a bloody nose.

"I don't know if the police can hold that tunnel," Beth said.

A rowdy group started to yell, "He's not our president!" They pushed back against the police, trying to move closer to Calvert

Station. It appeared that some men had weapons under their cloaks or coats.

Old Newton put a hand on Beth's shoulder. "You should leave," he said to the cousins. "The mayhem here is not for children."

Beth knew he was right. There was nothing she could do to keep Lincoln safe.

Patrick climbed down from the carriage first. He adjusted the hat. Beth hopped down too. She reached for the black bag on the seat. Just then, she saw a familiar face.

"Patrick, look!" Beth said. She pointed. Eugene was coming through the crowd. He had two policemen with him.

"Have you seen Captain Ferrandini?" Eugene asked the cousins when he drew near. "These police officers want to question him."

Patrick pointed. He said, "He and Mr. Hillard just went in that direction."

Beth hugged Eugene. He still looked like

an older teen. But it felt good to see a friendly face.

"Eugene—" she began.

"You mean, Mr. Davies," Eugene said.

"Yes," Beth said, "*Mr. Davies*. Will Mr. Lincoln be okay?"

A frown tugged at his lips. "History will take its course," he said. "I wasn't able to resume my acquaintance with Mr. Pinkerton or Mrs. Cherry in Philadelphia."

A flying bottle hit one of the police officers in the shoulder.

"Sorry, sir," the officer said to Eugene. "I can't look for this Ferrandini fellow. I've got to help control the crowd." The two police officers held their leather clubs high. They moved away from the carriage. They melted into the crowd, shouting for the people to stand back.

Patrick waved good-bye to Old Newton.

"Thank you for your help," Patrick said to the carriage driver.

Old Newton said, "Godspeed, my new young friends."

The cousins and Eugene pushed through people to reach an alley across from the station. Behind them, voices in the crowd seemed to grow angrier and angrier.

Beth heard a train whistle. She turned toward Calvert Station. "I have to go back," she said. "I have to know if Mr. Lincoln is on that train!"

The glow of the Imagination Station appeared. Soon the Model T stood nearby.

"According to historical documents, Lincoln should have made it through to Washington, DC," Eugene said. "It's time to return to Whit's End. Are you ready?"

"No!" Patrick said. "We still have Mr. Lincoln's inauguration speech. He'll need it if he lives long enough to give it."

Beth lifted the oilskin bag. "May we go to Washington?" she asked Eugene. "We'll either see Mr. Lincoln give the speech, or we'll be

there for his funeral."

"Very well," Eugene said.

This time Beth sat in the passenger seat. She held Lincoln's black bag tightly.

Patrick sat in the rumble seat. Eugene sat behind the steering wheel.

He slammed his fist into the red button.

*Blatt!*

**To find out about the next book in the series, *Rescue on the Combahee River,* visit TheImaginationStation.com.**

# Secret Word Puzzle

In Abraham Lincoln's day, telegrams were the fastest way to send information. After Mr. Lincoln left the Jones House hotel in Harrisburg, Pennsylvania, a friend sent a telegram to Allan Pinkerton. The telegram contained code words that told what time Mr. Lincoln's carriage had left the hotel. After the message was sent, the telegraph lines were cut.

Below is the Morse code alphabet, which was used in telegrams. The circles represent a short tap. The dashes represent a signal three times longer than a tap. Figure out the code below by filling in the blanks with the corresponding letters. Then you'll know the message. (The secret word is the one in boxes, and it's also the code name for Abraham Lincoln.)

FOCUS ON THE FAMILY PRESENTS
THE IMAGINATION STATION

# THE KEY TO ADVENTURE LIES WITHIN YOUR IMAGINATION.

1 VOYAGE WITH THE VIKINGS
2 ATTACK AT THE ARENA
3 PERIL IN THE PALACE
4 REVENGE OF THE RED KNIGHT
5 SHOWDOWN WITH THE SHEPHERD
6 PROBLEMS IN PLYMOUTH
7 SECRET OF THE PRINCE'S TOMB
8 BATTLE FOR CANNIBAL ISLAND
9 ESCAPE TO THE HIDING PLACE
10 CHALLENGE ON THE HILL OF FIRE
11 HUNT FOR THE DEVIL'S DRAGON
12 DANGER ON A SILENT NIGHT
13 THE REDCOATS ARE COMING!
14 CAPTURED ON THE HIGH SEAS
15 SURPRISE AT YORKTOWN
16 DOOMSDAY IN POMPEII
17 IN FEAR OF THE SPEAR
18 TROUBLE ON THE ORPHAN TRAIN
19 LIGHT IN THE LIONS' DEN
20 INFERNO IN TOKYO
21 MADMAN IN MANHATTAN
22 FREEDOM AT THE FALLS
23 TERROR IN THE TUNNEL

OVER 750,000 SOLD IN SERIES

COLLECT ALL OF THEM TODAY!

# AVAILABLE AT A CHRISTIAN RETAILER NEAR YOU

WWW.TYNDALE.COM

CP0874